Don Quixote

Written by Will Jamieson / Based on characters by Miguel de Cervantés

CARAMEL TREE

CARAMEL TREE
www.carameltree.com

Caramel Tree Readers | Level 6

Title: Don Quixote
Written by Will Jamieson / Illustrated by Melissa Lee / Based on characters by Miguel de Cervantés

Word count: 7,007
Lexile®: 650L

ISBN: 9788966293353
Copyright © JLS Co. Ltd. 2014

Published by JLS Co. Ltd. Offices in Vancouver BC, Seattle WA, and Seoul, Korea.

This book was printed in January 2014 by Mediaplus, #813-1, Galhyun-ri, Tanhyun-myun, Paju-si, Gyeonggi-do, Korea
1 4 0 1 0 3 2 0 1 8 0 6

Printed and manufactured in Korea

Don Quixote

Written by Will Jamieson / Based on characters by Miguel de Cervantés

CARAMEL TREE

CHAPTER 1

Daydreaming

"**A**ntonia, where are my gloves?" shouted the old man. "Antonia, Antonia! I need my gloves. NOW!"

"But it's so warm today, Señor Alonso? Why do you need gloves?" asked the young maid as she tried to reason with her master.

"I must have gloves," demanded Señor Alonso. "All French musketeers wear gloves."

"But we live in Spain where it is warm all year long, Señor," Antonia tried to explain. "And you are..." she hesitated, "you are not a French musketeer, sir. You are a retired Spanish farmer!" She picked up the book the old man was reading and waved it at him.

Señor Alonso looked at the book cover and smiled at the young maid. He had been daydreaming again.

The truth is that Señor Alonso was known to have a wild and creative imagination. He spent most of his time reading in his library and escaping into other worlds; the worlds of the stories he read. His favorite books were always about adventure. He liked books about sailors and pirates and giant whales. And he liked books about knights and castles and fearsome dragons. Sometimes he would spend the whole day sitting in his big brown chair, reading adventure stories, and drifting away into daydreams.

Señor Alonso lived alone on a large estate in a little town not far from the sea called La Mancha. He was rich. He had made his fortune shipping his famous peaches to far away countries. But he was now retired, never having married, and he relied on his four loyal servants for almost all his daily needs. He had a cook, a middle-aged man called Pedro, who made sure the old man ate well. He had two cleaning ladies for his huge mansion, the young Antonia and the older Maria. And there was Sancho, the round-bellied sleepy gardener, who took care of the garden and the stable.

Luckily, the four loyal servants were well aware of their master's wild imagination and they often had to deal with strange situations. Once, Antonia and Maria had to spend the whole day cleaning up animal droppings around the mansion because Señor Alonso had brought all sorts of animals into the house and behaved as if he could talk to them. On another occasion, all four loyal servants spent a whole afternoon pretending that their master was a giant. They crawled around on their knees and by the end of the afternoon, the two older servants, Pedro and Maria, could hardly stand up. Of course, these situations always arose from the stories Señor Alonso was reading.

One day, Señor Alonso sat in his big brown chair with an open book on his lap. His long skinny legs were stretched out with his feet on the table. He brushed his pointy beard with one hand. His other hand held the book open. The page had a picture of a knight on a big white horse, holding a sword high in the air. Señor Alonso was looking out the window. He was far away, daydreaming again.

"Señor Alonso?" asked a concerned voice.

Señor Alonso awoke from his daydream. Antonia was standing in the doorway. "Are you okay, sir?"

"Ah... yes, Antonia," responded a slightly confused Señor Alonso.

"I called you three times, but you didn't answer. Lunch is ready. It's beef stew, your favorite."

"Thank you, Antonia. I'll be right there."

Yawning, Señor Alonso closed his book. He stretched as he stood up and walked towards the door. He paused for a moment and then looked back to the window, smiled to himself, and went downstairs for lunch.

CHAPTER 2

A Knight

SLURP! SLURRP! Señor Alonso finished off the rest of his stew, dropped his spoon in his bowl with a loud clang, and wiped his mouth with his shirt sleeve.

"Ah! That was excellent, Pedro!" Señor Alonso said in a loud voice.

"I'm glad you enjoyed it, sir," said Pedro. He was staring at Señor Alonso who had a confused look on his face.

"Are you okay, sir? You are acting very strange today," said Pedro. He looked at Antonia and Maria who were clearing the table. They also seemed concerned.

Señor Alonso sat up straight and had a very serious look on

his face. "Antonia, Maria, Pedro. I have an announcement to make," Señor Alonso said in an important sounding voice.

Antonia, Maria, and Pedro looked at each other and didn't say anything.

"I have decided to become a knight."

"A knight?" asked Antonia. "You mean like from a fairytale? What are you talking about, sir?"

"I have decided to become a knight," Señor Alonso repeated. "You see, long ago, there were many knights. They traveled to many lands fighting robbers, helping the poor, and rescuing people from danger. They had many great adventures. They stood for honor and justice. I wish to do the same. I will be a knight."

Antonia started to laugh, but when she saw her master wasn't laughing, she realized he wasn't joking.

"Señor Alonso, are you serious? What about the house?" asked Maria.

"And what about your library?" asked Pedro.

"A knight has no need of such things," said Señor Alonso. "I will travel the countryside, helping those in need. I will eat what

I find and sleep where I can. People will write about my great adventures in books. They will call me..." Señor Alonso paused and looked out the window. "They will call me... Don Quixote."

"Don Quixote? That sounds very fancy, sir," said Antonia.

"Yes, Don Quixote of La Mancha. I will be a great hero like the knights of long ago."

"Hero? What..." Maria shook her head. She didn't know what to say. She turned to Antonia and Pedro and winked.

The old Señor Alonso stood up and ran out the door. Antonia, Maria and Pedro seemed worried but they knew that the best thing to do was to play along. Sooner or later Señor Alonso would come back to his senses and come back home. At least they hoped he would.

CHAPTER 3

Silver

"Wake up, Sancho! Your master needs you." The old man shook the gardener's leg.

Sancho opened his eyes, shook his big round head, and looked around. "Yes, Señor Alonso. How can I help you?" asked sleepy Sancho as he rubbed his eyes.

"I am Don Quixote of La Mancha," said Señor Alonso. "From now on, you must call me Don Quixote!"

Sancho looked up at his master and scratched his big round belly. He had fallen asleep in the grass and had dirt and leaves stuck to his face. "Don Quixote?" asked confused Sancho as he sat up.

"Yes! Don Quixote," said the old man.

"Excuse me, Señor... I mean Don Quixote," Sancho corrected himself.

"Yes! Don Quixote." The old man stood tall. "Sancho, my good man, I come to you with good news. Today is a great day! We are leaving on a great adventure to faraway lands to fight for honor and justice. You will be my companion on this great journey," announced Don Quixote in a loud voice.

Sancho nodded slowly, unsure of what was going on, and stood up.

"I say, Sancho, they will write books about our great adventures. Our journey will be famous!"

"Are we going to the market in La Mancha, sir?" asked Sancho.

"No, you silly hairy man! We are off to unknown lands to help those in need!" yelled Don Quixote.

"Of course, sir," answered Sancho. Now that he was awake, he took a closer look at his master whom he had noticed was looking very different today. He was wearing a rusty suit of armor which was clearly too small for him. He was also wearing a knight's helmet and carrying a long pointed stick that looked like a lance. "Excuse me, sir, but why are you dressed like that, sir? Is there a costume party today?"

"I am dressed as the Great Knight, Don Quixote, the hero of La Mancha! We will have many great adventures and when we return, you my friend, will be rewarded with... an island!"

"An island? Thank you, sir," Sancho smiled. He was not very smart. Although the promise of having his own island excited him, he was a little unsure how his master could give him an island.

"Get up, Sancho! We must find two great horses for our journey," announced Don Quixote.

Sancho stood up, still confused, but a little excited. He followed his master to the stable where there were four donkeys.

The estate had once had many horses, but over the years, they had either died or been sold. Now, all that was left in the stable were three brown donkeys and one gray donkey.

"Ummm...," Sancho hesitated, but he knew that he had to play along with his master. "Which one do you like?" Sancho showed his master the four donkeys.

Don Quixote slowly inspected the donkeys.

As they came to the gray donkey, Don Quixote stopped and smiled. "I'll take this one! This is a knight's horse," he said.

"You don't want this one, sir. He's always eating garbage and he has very bad gas," Sancho explained. He didn't dare correct his master by saying that it was a donkey, not a horse.

"This is a knight's horse," Don Quixote continued. "I will call him, Silver!"

PRRRRRT... came a sound from the donkey's behind followed by a terrible smell.

"You see, sir, very bad gas," repeated Sancho.

Not seeming to notice, Don Quixote took Silver out of the barn and climbed on top of him. "Come, Sancho! Adventure is waiting for us!" he yelled as he rode the lazy donkey down the road.

Sancho climbed onto his little brown donkey and followed his master.

CHAPTER 4

The Tomatoes

Don Quixote and Sancho rode all afternoon. They rode through the town of La Mancha where they received more than a few curious looks. Then they rode through the hills to the East. The sun was shining and there was a nice cool wind.

Late in the afternoon, they met an old farmer along the road. He was pulling a cart full of tomatoes. The old farmer waved to them politely as they were passing.

Don Quixote stopped Silver and climbed off. "Good day to you, fine sir," he said. "How are you on this beautiful afternoon?"

"I'm just fine, thank you. I'm taking my tomatoes to the next town to sell them at the market," answered the old farmer. "Say, why are you dressed like that?"

"I am the Great Knight, Don Quixote of La Mancha and this is my loyal companion, Sancho. We are on a great journey to help those in need. We fight for honor and justice. Is there anything we can do to help you today?" proclaimed Don Quixote in a loud voice.

"No, thank you. I'm quite alright," answered the old farmer. Then he added, "A knight, you say? I don't remember ever seeing a knight around here before."

"Yes, sir. A knight. I am the bravest knight in all of Spain. Are you sure there is nothing we can do to help you? You look very tired. Maybe we could use Silver, my strong horse, to pull your cart to the next town?" suggested Don Quixote.

The old farmer looked at Don Quixote and was unsure of what to think. He looked at Silver and was sure it was a donkey, not a horse. Then he looked at Sancho who was smiling politely. The old farmer was tired so he agreed to let Silver pull his cart to town.

"Excellent!" Don Quixote shouted. He was very happy at the thought of being able to help someone. "Sancho, tie Silver to this

man's cart. We will pull the tomatoes to town."

"Yes, sir." Sancho climbed off his donkey and tied Silver to the old man's cart.

"Well done, good Sancho. Now forward, Silver," said Don Quixote as he kicked Silver to make him walk. Silver stood still. "I say forward, Silver," ordered Don Quixote again as he kicked him harder. Silver looked up at him with big sleepy eyes and then down at the ground.

PRRRRRRT!...

"Oh, what's that smell?" asked the old farmer.

Don Quixote climbed off Silver and tried to pull him forward, but Silver just stood still looking at him. Don Quixote was getting angry. He turned and slapped Silver hard on his behind.

"Go, Silver!" he shouted.

Surprised, Silver let out a loud 'WEEE HEEE HEE!' jumped forward and started to run down the road. The cart followed him and bounced up and down on the bumpy road with fresh red tomatoes falling everywhere.

"Nooo! My tomatoes!" shouted the old farmer.

The three men chased Silver down the road slipping on

tomatoes as they ran. Suddenly, the rope pulling the cart broke, the cart went rolling off the road, and crashed into a tree. The cart flipped over and tomatoes flew everywhere.

The terrified old farmer could only watch. He walked over to his cart. It was missing two wheels and was upside down. His tomatoes were everywhere in a big squished red mess.

"You, idiots!" yelled the old farmer. "What have you done? What have you done!" he screamed. He was very angry.

"Ahh... well..." Don Quixote started. He and Sancho looked at each other.

"These were all my tomatoes! What will I sell now?"

"I'm very sorry, good sir," Don Quixote began, "but if you had bought a better cart, maybe we would not have had this problem."

The old farmer hit Sancho with his walking stick.

"Stupid! Stupid!" he yelled as he chased them down the road.

CHAPTER 5

The Play

The next day, Don Quixote and Sancho were riding through a quiet green forest. Sancho was rubbing his back where the old man had hit him.

"So, how big is this island of mine, sir?" he asked.

"It will be very big, good Sancho. And beautiful, covered in gardens for you to enjoy," answered Don Quixote.

"I've never heard of an island covered in gardens," said Sancho.

"That is because you are not a great knight, Sancho. There are many stories of garden-covered islands in my books. You will soon see, my simple friend," explained Don Quixote.

"But first, adventure awaits! We must save more people!" Don Quixote had a determined look on his face.

Sancho followed his master silently on their journey. They rode over a little hill and saw a small village on the other side of the hill. In the middle of the village, they could see a group of people sitting together. Then, they heard a girl's voice crying for help.

"Help! Please someone, save me from these mean scary robbers! Help! Help!" cried the girl.

"Listen good Sancho! A girl is in need of help! This is a job for the Great Don Quixote of La Mancha!" Don Quixote jumped off Silver and ran into the village square waving his lance in the air.

Sancho sat on his donkey and watched from the hill. He looked closer at the group of people in the middle of the village. He saw a young girl and three men who looked like robbers. They were on a stage. There was a group of people sitting on wooden chairs facing the stage... it was a play!

"Sir! Wait!" yelled Sancho as he chased after his master on his little brown donkey. But it was too late. Don Quixote was already leaping onto the stage.

"Let that girl go!" yelled Don Quixote as he jumped onto the stage. The actors all looked quite confused. The crowd clapped in excitement, but Don Quixote didn't seem to notice.

"Who are you?" asked one of the robbers. He was very surprised.

"I am the Great Knight, Don Quixote of La Mancha and you will let this poor girl go!" Don Quixote yelled as he waved his lance in the air and jumped on one of the actors.

The crowd cheered with excitement as Don Quixote fought with the three men who were all very surprised. Soon, Sancho jumped into the fight and tried to pull his master off from one of the robbers. He slipped and fell off the stage landing in the cheering crowd.

"What are you doing?" yelled the girl in the play as she tried to get between Don Quixote and the robbers.

Don Quixote spun around, bumped into the girl, and knocked her off the stage. She landed on Sancho as he was trying to stand up. They both fell back into the crowd.

The young girl stepped on Sancho's round belly as she stood back up. "Stop! Please stop!" she cried.

As the three confused robbers crawled off the stage, Don Quixote stopped fighting.

"Victory! Victory!" He shouted as he held his lance in the air. He turned to the young girl and bowed.

"My lady, you are safe now. I, Don Quixote of La Mancha, have rescued you from these evil robbers," he said in a very proud voice.

"Safe? What are you talking about? Can't you see we are actors? You ruined our play!"

"My lady... uh..." Don Quixote looked around. He saw the crowd, the stage, and the robbers in their costumes. "I'm very sorry... I thought... uh..."

"BOOO!" yelled someone in the crowd. Someone else threw an apple at Don Quixote, but it hit Sancho instead. Soon, everyone was yelling 'BOOO!' and throwing food at them.

"Quick, Sancho! We must get to our horses!"

The crowd chased Don Quixote as he ran away and jumped onto Silver. Sancho followed closely on his little brown donkey as the angry screaming crowd chased them and threw food and garbage at them.

CHAPTER 6

The Dragon

Don Quixote and Sancho were very tired from the fight at the village. Sancho's belly was sore where the young actress had stepped on him. But they continued on their journey for honor and justice across Spain.

One day, as they were riding through a field, Don Quixote suddenly stopped. He was looking at something in the distance.

Sancho rode up beside his master. "What is it, sir?"

"Look, Sancho! I can't believe it. I see a dragon!" Don Quixote pointed to the sky where a great colorful creature seemed to fly back and forth. It had a big mouth and a long tail. It was orange and green with bright red spots. As they watched the creature fly, Don Quixote gasped. "Oh, no! Sancho, Look!"

Don Quixote pointed at two boys standing below the flying dragon. They seemed to be watching the dragon fly back and forth.

"Sancho, the children are in danger! That terrible dragon will soon eat them if we do not protect them. This is a job for a great hero!"

Don Quixote kicked Silver and off he went racing across the field waving his lance above him. As he got closer, Don Quixote lifted his lance and began to yell as loud as he could.

"Do not fear, children! Don Quixote of La Mancha, the Great Knight, will protect you from this evil creature! Prepare to die, you terrible dragon!" shouted Don Quixote. He lifted his lance and threw it as hard as he could at the dragon. The lance flew through the air and struck the dragon bringing it crashing down.

"Yeehaaa!" Don Quixote yelled as he neared the creature and jumped on top of it. He picked up his lance and beat the dragon over and over until it stopped moving. Then, he fell to the ground exhausted.

"Victory! Yes...Victory! I can't... believe it!... I killed... a...

dragon!" Don Quixote shouted out of breath. He was very tired

but also very happy.

When surprised Sancho finally caught up with him, he

climbed off his donkey and looked at the 'dragon.' It was a

dragon, alright. A big colorful dragon... kite.

The dragon kite had a big hole in the middle of it made by

the lance. It was destroyed.

Sancho looked at the two boys. Both of them were in shock.

The smaller boy walked over to the kite and stared at it. He

sniffed a couple of times and then he started to cry.

"Waaaaa! Why did you break our kite? Waaaaaaaa!" cried

the boy.

"Do not cry, boy," said Don Quixote, still lying on the ground

trying to catch his breath. "You have been saved by the Great

Don Quixote of La Mancha! Killer of dragons! Hero of Spain!"

He slowly sat up.

The boy cried louder and louder. "Mommy! The bad man

broke my dragon!"

"Why did you break my little brother's birthday present,

mister? And what are you wearing?" asked the other boy.

Don Quixote looked down at the 'dragon' he had just killed. His face changed when he saw it was just a kite.

"My master thought he was saving you from a dragon," said Sancho. "We are very sorry."

"Waaaaaa!" cried the smaller boy. "I want a new dragon."

"I'm very sorry, little boy," said Don Quixote, trying to put the broken kite back together.

"I'm going to tell my mommy you broke my dragon, you mean man!" said the boy angrily. His face was very red.

"No, no, no. You don't need to tell anyone about this. What if I gave you a new birthday present?" Don Quixote asked the boy. "Would you like our pony?"

The boy slowly stopped crying and wiped his tears away with his hand. He looked at Don Quixote, then at Sancho, sniffing. "A pony?" said the boy finally.

Don Quixote pointed at Sancho's little brown donkey.

"Sir?" asked very surprised Sancho. "OUR pony?"

The boys stopped crying and walked over to Sancho's little brown donkey. They had never seen a pony before so they believed the little brown donkey was a pony.

Sancho sighed and gave them his pony.

As Don Quixote and Sancho rode away on Silver, they looked back at the two boys running and playing with the pony in the field.

"Well, at least we still have good old Silver," said Don Quixote.

"Yes, sir," answered Sancho.

PRRRRRT! Silver let out some gas. Carrying two people was heavy work.

CHAPTER 7

The Baker

That night, Don Quixote and Sancho slept under a tree beside a river. In the morning, Sancho cooked a fish he had caught in the river for breakfast. "Would you like some breakfast sir?" Sancho offered his master some of the fish and a piece of bread.

"Thank you, good Sancho," Don Quixote said as he took a big bite. "What I would give for some of Pedro's delicious beef stew right now! I very much miss our home in La Mancha."

"Me, too, sir!" Sancho was hoping his master would finally decide to go back home.

"But a knight must be strong when he is on a long journey

for honor and justice. Is this not true?"

"Yes, sir, very true," answered loyal Sancho. His hopes for a speedy return home were crushed. "But we need to buy some more bread today. We have eaten all the bread we brought with us."

"Maybe there is a bakery in the next town," said Don Quixote.

The two men ate breakfast and then set off down the road. By the afternoon, they came to a small quiet town. It was very much like La Mancha, but a little bit smaller. There were very few people on the street. The people were looking at the two men with great interest. They were smiling and laughing at the two men riding on Silver.

"These people look very friendly," said Don Quixote. "Let's ask someone where the bakery is, Sancho."

The two men stopped in the middle of town.

"Excuse me, sir," Sancho asked a man walking by. "Is there a bakery in town?"

"Just around the corner," said the man smiling broadly.

They thanked the man and rode Silver to a building around the corner. They climbed off Silver and tied him to a tree outside.

As they went inside, they were surprised to find no bread. Don Quixote and Sancho looked around the room. There were a few books on a shelf and a desk with some papers on it. There didn't seem to be any people inside the building.

"Hello? Is anyone here?" cried Don Quixote.

"Yes, in the back!" yelled a voice.

The two men walked to the back of the building and saw a skinny man in what looked like a closet with a door made of iron bars. The skinny man was smiling and waving to them from behind the bars. He had a gold tooth that shined when he smiled.

"Is this the town bakery, good sir?" asked Don Quixote.

"Um... yes, this is the town bakery," answered the skinny man. "Welcome! How may I help you today?"

"I am the Great Knight, Don Quixote of La Mancha and this is my loyal companion, Sancho. We have traveled across many lands for honor and justice. We want to buy some bread for our journey."

"Yes, of course... you are a great knight," said the skinny man as he looked back and forth between Don Quixote and Sancho.

"If this is the town bakery, where is all the bread?" asked Sancho looking around the room.

"The bread... yes... the bread," said the skinny man as he nervously scratched his ear. "It's a very funny story. You see, I was cleaning the closet here so I could put some bread in it. But I accidentally locked myself inside! I feel so foolish," the skinny man laughed.

"Ah yes, foolish indeed, sir," answered Don Quixote.

"If you are not too busy Great Knight, with your great journey for honor and justice, would you please help me get out of this closet so I might get you some bread for your travels?" the skinny man asked with a big smile.

"Good baker, today is a very lucky day for you. Don Quixote of La Mancha has come to rescue you. Where is the key to this strange iron closet you have foolishly locked yourself in?"

"The key is on the desk in the front of the bakery," said the skinny man. He seemed very excited about getting out of the closet.

"Go find this key, my loyal Sancho!" ordered Don Quixote.

"But, sir, maybe we should wait and..." Sancho began.

"Quickly, Sancho!" Don Quixote interrupted. "We must help this poor trapped baker so he can return to his baking."

Sancho went to the front room and returned with the key which he gave to Don Quixote. Don Quixote put the key in the lock, turned it, and opened the door. The skinny man was smiling and very excited.

"You are free, good baker. Great Knight, Don Quixote of La Mancha has rescued you from this closet and your own foolishness. Now, if you could please bring us some bread we..."

As Don Quixote was still talking, the man ran out of the closet, out of the room, and then out the front door. He seemed to be laughing as he ran. Don Quixote looked at Sancho with surprise.

"Where do you think he is going, sir? Do you think he keeps his bread somewhere else?" asked Sancho.

"Sancho, my silly friend, you do not know anything about rescuing people," Don Quixote explained. "This poor foolish baker is so happy to be rescued by a great knight that he has gone to find his friends and neighbors so that they might have a party to honor us and bring us gifts."

"Gifts, sir?"

"Yes, Sancho. Great, beautiful, and expensive gifts," Don Quixote went on. "You see, many years ago, people would give knights, like myself, great gifts to thank them for rescuing them from danger. This man is so happy not to be lost forever in his strange iron closet, that he..."

Don Quixote stopped talking as another man entered the room. He was wearing a blue hat, a blue uniform, and he had a sword. He was a policeman. "Who are you?" he asked.

"I am the Great Knight, Don Quixote of La Mancha. We are on a journey for..."

"How did you get in here?" yelled the policeman. "And where is my prisoner?"

"Your prisoner?" Don Quixote began. He looked confused. "If you are speaking of the good baker, he has gone to bring us gifts. He wants to thank us for rescuing him from..."

"Rescue? What have you done!" cried the policeman.

"We have saved the poor baker from that strange iron closet in the back of the bakery. He left several minutes ago," answered Don Quixote.

"You idiots!" yelled the policeman. "That man you helped escape is the most famous thief in all of Spain! It took me two years to catch him and now he is gone!"

"Thief? We thought... ah..." Don Quixote tried to explain.

"Idiots! Which way did he go?" yelled the policeman.

Don Quixote pointed out the door and tried to speak but before he could say anything, the policeman ran out the door and down the street. He was looking in doors and windows as he ran. As he disappeared around a corner, they could still hear him yelling 'Idiots!'

Don Quixote looked at the ground. He still looked confused. He looked up when Sancho spoke.

"Sir," said Sancho. "Silver is gone."

CHAPTER 8

The Chickens

It took them many days to walk back to La Mancha. They walked through fields and forests. They walked through mountains and over hills. Near the end, they were so tired from walking that they stopped and sat on the side of the road. Finally, a man passed by with a cart full of chickens and was kind enough to give them a ride.

The Great Knight, Don Quixote sat in the cart with his loyal friend Sancho covered in dust and dirt and chickens. When they finally reached La Mancha, they climbed out of the cart, thanked the man with the chickens, and walked the long road to the estate.

When Antonia opened the door, she could hardly believe she was looking at her master. He was dirty and tired and covered in chicken feathers.

"Señor Alonso!" cried Antonia. "Look, Señor Alonso and Sancho have returned," she called the other servants.

Pedro and Maria came running and stopped when they saw their master. They could not believe their eyes.

"Sir! What happened to you!" gasped Maria. She held her apron over her nose. He smelled terrible.

The old man did not say anything. He just looked down and walked silently into his house.

"Pedro! Quick, bring Señor Alonso some food!" said Antonia.

Pedro ran to the kitchen and came back with a bowl of beef stew. He tried to give it to Don Quixote, but he did not take it. The old man's spirit was crushed. The tired old man just mumbled to himself as he slowly walked upstairs into his bedroom, dropped onto his bed, and fell fast asleep.

CHAPTER **9**

The Plan

That night after dinner, Sancho told everyone the story of their great journey across Spain. He told them about the old farmer they had tried to help and how all of his tomatoes were squished. He told them about the play and how the actors and the angry crowd had chased them out of the village. He told them about the two boys with their dragon kite and how they had lost the little brown *pony*. He told them about the famous thief they thought was a baker and how the policeman had been very angry. Finally, he told them how they had walked for many days through fields and forests and mountains and hills then rode in a chicken cart all the way back to La Mancha. He was

very tired when he finished telling the story.

When Sancho had finished, Antonia, Maria, and Pedro sat staring at each other. They could not believe how the great journey for honor and justice had turned out so badly.

"Poor Señor Alonso!" said Antonia as she began to cry. "All he wanted to do was to help people."

"Yes," Sancho shook his head. "It would have been nice if he could have helped just one person. If he could have helped someone or saved one person from danger, I think he would feel better. Everywhere we went, people laughed at us and called us 'idiots.' They even threw food and garbage at us."

"Maybe we can give Señor Alonso one adventure to be proud of," said Pedro.

"What do you mean, Pedro?" asked Antonia.

"Maybe we could make up an adventure for Señor Alonso. We could give him someone to rescue so that he would have something to be proud of again," Pedro explained.

"What a great idea!" said Maria. "How could we do this?"

Antonia, Maria, and Sancho stayed up late drinking tea and listening to Pedro as he explained his plan. When he was finished explaining, they all went to bed.

CHAPTER **10**

The Princess

KNOCK! KNOCK!

"Sir! Wake up sir!" cried Sancho as he banged on his master's bedroom door. He waited for a moment but no one answered. He tried again.

KNOCK! KNOCK!

"Sir, please wake up! I need your help!" Sancho cried even louder.

"Go away," answered the old man. "I just want to sleep all day."

KNOCK! KNOCK! KNOCK!

"Please, sir! You cannot sleep all day! We must leave soon," Sancho tried again.

"I'm not going anywhere!" cried the old man. "I'm the worst knight who has ever lived! I just want to be left alone so I can sleep all day. Now, go away, Sancho!"

Sancho started to slowly walk away from the door as he scratched his big round belly. Then he stopped, turned around, and went back to the door.

KNOCK! KNOCK! KNOCK! KNOCK!

He took a deep breath.

"I have come for the Great Knight, Don Quixote of La Mancha!" Sancho shouted in a proud voice. "I, the loyal Sancho, have been sent by the King of Spain to find my great master!

Something terrible has happened and Spain needs its greatest and most famous knight! Will you come with me Don Quixote? For honor and for justice?"

Sancho stopped talking and took another deep breath. He stood quietly in the hall and waited. Then, very slowly, the door opened.

"...Yes?" his master asked quietly.

"Don Quixote, you must come with me. A princess has been taken prisoner by an evil knight and a terrible witch! They have taken her and locked her in a castle by the sea! The king has sent me to find you so that we might rescue this poor girl," Sancho explained.

"Rescue a princess?" Don Quixote was starting to look himself again.

"Yes, sir. She needs our help."

"Rescue a princess! Of course! Sancho, we must go now! Bring me my armor and my lance!"

Sancho ran to get his master's things. Don Quixote quickly put on his armor and picked up his lance. Sancho was very happy to see his master back to his old self again.

"There is some good news, sir," said Sancho as they were walking out the door. "Last night, our friend Silver returned. He must have escaped from the thief and returned home. He is waiting outside."

"Wonderful, Sancho! That is very good news!" shouted Don Quixote.

This was not true of course. That morning, Sancho had taken one of the two remaining brown donkeys and covered it with soot to make it look gray. Don Quixote didn't even notice.

The two men climbed onto the animal and then Don Quixote kicked it to make it run. "Away Silver! We must save a princess!"

The Great Knight, Don Quixote held his lance in the air as they rode away.

CHAPTER *11*

The Evil Knight
and the Terrible Witch

Don Quixote and his loyal companion, Sancho, rode all afternoon and then into the evening. By the time they reached the sea, it was getting dark and starting to rain. Finally, Sancho spotted the place Pedro had told him. It was a small inn by the seaside. He could see the light of a fire inside the inn.

"There, sir! That's the castle the king said belongs to the evil knight. That is where the evil knight and the terrible witch are keeping the princess!" Sancho explained pointing to the little inn.

"Indeed, Sancho. We must go quickly," said Don Quixote as he scratched his long pointy beard. He did not doubt that the place was a castle as Sancho had pointed out.

Don Quixote and Sancho walked down to the beach as the rain poured down on them.

"Here, sir," shouted Sancho pointing at the side entrance to the inn. "This is the secret entrance to the castle!"

Suddenly, lightning flashed and they heard the sound of thunder not too far away.

Above them through a window, Pedro, Maria, and Antonia watched. Pedro was wearing a black knight's helmet and was carrying a wooden sword. Maria was dressed like a witch. Pedro had given her a carrot to stick on her nose to make it look ugly. Antonia was dressed like a princess and had her face covered with a scarf.

"Here they come!" whispered Pedro through his helmet. "Everyone get ready!"

CHAPTER 12

The Rescue

"Ha Ha Ha! Where is your treasure, princess!" shouted Pedro as loud as he could so that Don Quixote would hear. "You *will* give us your gold."

"Yes, give us your gold you silly little princess! Hee Hee Hee!" Maria screamed in an evil witch's voice.

They were all trying very hard not to laugh. Below them, Don Quixote stopped and listened. He waved to Sancho to come closer.

"Did you hear that, Sancho?" he whispered. "That poor princess is up there. We must get ready to fight!"

As they quietly walked up the stairs, they heard them speak again.

"I am not afraid of you!" shouted Antonia in her best princess voice. "The king has sent for the greatest knight in all of Spain to rescue me. Have you heard of him? His name is Don Quixote."

"Ahhh! Not Don Quixote!" the witch screamed. "Anyone but him! He is the most famous knight in all of Spain!"

"Yes," shouted Pedro. "I have heard of him, too. He fights for honor and for justice! What will we do?"

"I'm scared!" screamed Maria in her witch's voice.

Below them, Don Quixote was smiling excitedly. He turned to Sancho and signaled. "After I kick the door open, we will attack. Are you ready, good Sancho?"

"Yes, sir!"

Don Quixote kicked the door open. Maria, the witch screamed loudly and ran to hide behind Pedro, the evil knight. Pedro lifted his wooden sword and ran towards Don Quixote.

"Attack!" yelled Don Quixote.

Antonia hid in the corner behind her scarf and watched as Don Quixote, Sancho, Pedro, and Maria chased each other around the room screaming and yelling. They hit each other with sticks and brooms. They jumped off of chairs and threw things at each other. The whole time, Antonia laughed quietly to herself behind her scarf.

After about twenty minutes of screaming, yelling, throwing things, and hitting each other, Pedro ran towards the door with his wooden sword in the air.

"Run away! Run away!" he shouted. "This great knight is too strong! Run away!"

Maria ran out the door and down the stairs screaming and crying, and Pedro followed closely behind her. Don Quixote continued to swing his lance in the air for a bit longer accidentally hitting Sancho several times. Then, he slowly looked around and realized the evil knight and the witch were gone. He smiled at Sancho and lifted his lance in the air.

"Victory! Victory!" he shouted. "We have won, Sancho! Victory!"

Antonia ran to Don Quixote and hugged him.

"Thank you brave knight! Thank you so much! All of Spain thanks you," she said with great happiness. "You are a great knight and a hero. You have rescued me!"

"It is my honor, my lady," said a very tired Don Quixote as he fell down in a chair. "For I am the Great Knight, Don Quixote of La Mancha and I fight for... for..."

As he was still speaking, Don Quixote fell fast asleep in the chair.

CHAPTER **13**

Loyalty

Vhen Don Quixote woke up the next morning, he was in his bed. Loyal Sancho had carried him home on the back of the donkey, which was brown again since the rain had washed away the soot. Don Quixote had slept the whole time. Pedro, Maria, and Antonia had sneaked back to the estate that night and changed out of their costumes.

When Don Quixote came downstairs for breakfast, everyone was waiting for him at the kitchen table.

"Good morning, sir," Antonia said. "Sancho was just telling us about your great adventure last night. We are all very proud of you!"

"Thank you, Antonia," Don Quixote answered cheerfully.

"You should have seen him fight that evil knight and that terrible witch," said Sancho. "I've never seen anyone fight so bravely."

"Oh, it was nothing special," Don Quixote smiled as he had a sip of his tea. "I just did what any good knight would do."

"I can't believe that you are a great and famous knight, sir!" Antonia said with her hands on her cheeks.

"Well, not anymore," said a tired Don Quixote. "I have had many great adventures and traveled to many lands, but I'm just too tired to fight anymore. I just want to read in my library and stay at home close to you, my loyal friends."

They all looked at each other quite surprised.

Don Quixote stood up and walked towards his library then stopped and turned around.

"Oh, by the way my good Sancho, I am going to buy you the little island with the castle."

Sancho opened his mouth and tried to speak, but nothing came out. Then, he stood up and put his hand over his heart.

"It has been a great honor to serve you, Don Quixote of La Mancha."

Don Quixote smiled.

"Call me Alonso, my friend," he said as he walked to his library.

Caramel Tree Readers

Our books are published across seven levels, so young readers at every level can find the perfect books for them.

Level	Words*	Lexile® Measures
S Starter	50 to 100	Up to 300L

Alphabet and Phonics picture books with songs that help lay the foundations for reading

| **1** Beginner | 200 | 100L to 350L |

Fully illustrated themed stories with easy words and plenty of picture clues

| **2** Elementary | 500 | 200L to 500L |

Illustrated fairy tale adaptations with short sentences and unique twists

| **3** Pre-Intermediate | 1000 | 300L to 600L |

Easy to follow plots with the 'Magic 1000 words' in various settings and up to twenty full page illustrations

| **4** Intermediate | 2000 | 400L to 700L |

Character-based stories that help readers explore themes for personal growth

| **5** Upper-Intermediate | 4000 | 500L to 800L |

Action-packed stories with multiple characters and clear problem/resolution arcs

| **6** Advanced | 7000 | 550L to 900L |

Classic story adaptations and new stories with longer chapters and more complex plots

Señor Alonso is an old retired farmer. He constantly reads adventure books about knights of honor and justice, and soon starts to believe they are true. The old man changes his name to Don Quixote of La Mancha, the most famous knight in Spain. He takes his loyal servant, Sancho, with him on many failed adventures, but finds redemption in the cleverly devised planning of his house servants.

Level	Lexile®
S Starter	Up to 300L
1 Beginner	100L to 350L
2 Elementary	200L to 500L
3 Pre-Intermediate	300L to 600L
4 Intermediate	400L to 700L
5 Upper-Intermediate	500L to 800L
6 Advanced	550L to 900L

Caramel Tree Readers are carefully graded using The Lexile® Framework for Reading, providing a gradual progression across seven levels from Starter to Advanced. Each level offers a delicious range of stories with beautiful illustrations, engaging plots, and memorable characters. Visit our website to learn more about Caramel Tree Readers and to find the perfect storybooks for young readers of every level.

LEXILE®

CARAMEL TREE
Delicious English

www.carameltree.com

ISBN 9788966293353

US $5.99
CAN $6.99
5 0 5 9 9

9 788966 293353